Dogball

First published in 2008
by Wayland

This paperback edition published in 2009

Wayland
338 Euston Road
London NW1 3BH

Wayland Australia
Level 17/207 Kent Street
Sydney, NSW 2000

Series Editor: Louise John
Editor: Katie Powell
Cover design: Paul Cherrill
Design: D.R.ink
Consultant: Shirley Bickler

A CIP catalogue record for this book is available from the British Library.

ISBN 9780750255240 (hbk)
ISBN 9780750255257 (pbk)

Printed in China

Wayland is a division of Hachette Children's Books,
an Hachette Livre UK Company

www.hachettelivre.co.uk

Dogball

Written by Pippa Goodhart
Illustrated by Sue Mason

WAYLAND

The class was getting dressed
for PE.

"That's my sock!" said Nasim.
"No, it's mine!" said Bella.

Nasim and Bella both pulled.
Bump! Bella let go and Nasim
landed on Miss Samson.

Miss Samson put her hands on her hips. "Out you go!" she said. "We'll do some races."

"Can we play football?
Please?" said Jake.
"I hate running races."

"OK," said Miss Samson.
"We'll play football."
"Hooray!" everybody shouted.

Out on the field, they got
ready to play.

Miss Samson put the ball
down and blew her whistle.

Jake lifted his leg,
ready to kick off.

Just then, a dog ran over and took the ball!

"Hey, you!" shouted Jake. "Stop!"

Off ran the dog,
and Jake followed.

So did Bella, Nasim and all the others.

They ran across the field...

...but they couldn't catch the dog.

They ran – splish splash –
through puddles.

They ran – slip slide –
through mud.

They ran – crunch crunch –
over stones.

The dog ran.

Bella ran.

Nasim ran.

But Jake had stopped.
He was too puffed to
keep running.

"Wait for me!" he shouted.

Just then, the dog ran past Jake. This time it was going the other way.

"Hey, you!" shouted Jake
and he began to run again.

The dog ran back to
the field and sat down.

Jake got there first.
"I've got him!" shouted Jake.
"And I've got the ball!"

"Well done, Jake!" said
Miss Samson.

She looked at the dog's
name-tag.
"And well done, Pogo!"

"You ran a race after all!"
laughed Miss Samson.
"Jake is the winner!"

"I've never won a race before!" Jake smiled. "What do I win?"

"You can choose what we play next," said Miss Samson.

"Choose football!" shouted the class. But Jake shook his head.

"I choose we play
DOGBALL!" he said.

START READING is a series of highly enjoyable books for beginner readers. **The books have been carefully graded to match the Book Bands widely used in schools.** This enables readers to be sure they choose books that match their own reading ability.

Look out for the Band colour on the book in our Start Reading logo.

The Bands are:

Pink Band 1

Red Band 2

Yellow Band 3

Blue Band 4

Green Band 5

Orange Band 6

Turquoise Band 7

Purple Band 8

Gold Band 9

START READING books can be read independently or shared with an adult. They promote the enjoyment of reading through satisfying stories supported by fun illustrations.

Pippa Goodhart lives with her husband, three daughters, a dog, a cat and four chickens who all leave interesting footprints on her floors. She found learning to read hard, but now loves reading, and writing, books.

Sue Mason grew up in East Sussex, surrounded by trees, eating crumpets. She illustrates from a happy little studio called The Chocolate Factory, which she shares with special friends. Sometimes they break from work to have a little dance around and eat cake.